Howl of Conquest

Tyler Morley

Contents

Chapter 1

Werewolf and Lycan Rules:

1. Lycans can mask their scent if they do choose.

2. Mates can be found through scent and eye contact as long as the scent isn't masked.

3. Lycans pups develop fast. 1 year is about 2 for a Lycan pup.

4. Abilities are gene specific but can develop into other abilities. Elemental, demonic, telepathy and so on.

5. The wolf and human are separate entities but both share primal needs, such as hunting, mating and such.

6. Pups born outside of a mated pair are normally frowned upon in Lycan and werewolf society.

7. Lycans and werewolf forms are 2 separate forms.

8. Becoming the next alpha is blood passed not by defeat unless a challenge is presented and whoever submits wins. Murder does not pass the leadership.

Chapter 2

1^{900} In a time where being a beast was crucial to existing among many Predators. The most primal instincts were embraced. To protect from human hunters, vampire covens and other creatures.5 clans lived among each other in peace. Trading good, sharing survival skills and defending each other from any threats. 2 royal lycan clans from the original bloodlines, 2 separate bloodlines on separate parts on the world moved into Ireland to create order and law. To be close to one another. These creatures stood on 2 feet, the speed of their movement was unmatchable as well as their ability to hunt. Great strength and immortality were only 2 of their cursed gifts. Night meadow had a ruthless alpha and Luna. Feared by many and were not known for patience. Very firm in their viking beliefs that kept the pack safe. Among there incredible strength they bear the curse of the dark. The power to bring forth a buried demonic monster within themselves to subdue and who dare face them. Alpha Augustus Sage and Luna Syvia Sage were a force one should never attempt cross.

Then there were the Celtics beasts. Alpha Lorance Astair was voted to be king due to their fierce nature when it came to their kind, which balanced with kindness. No wolf would go hungry or live in filth. The love for the packs was evident, his mate Autumn had a heart bigger that Ireland itself, her kind nature turned to pure rage when her pack was suffering. A true mother. These Royals were gifted in many more ways. They possess the gifts of the elements, earth, air, fire and water could be controlled by these beasts of the night.

The other 3 clans belonged to the werewolves. Although ancestors of the lycans these clans began to change the more they bred away from the royal line, putting them on 4 legs. This gave them a greater advantage. Warriors were born and trained in these clans. Smaller, faster and more able to move into small areas. Blood curse pack had a selfish alpha Zander Stiles, he took many women with or without consent all the while his Luna writhed in hell from his infidelity. Silent hunt was run by his close friend Wendell Pike. These 2 men did a lot of under the radar trading such as women and children. Unbearable acts ruined the love in their packs.

On the opposite side of Ireland was alpha Bruin Maximus accompanied by Luna Sky and beautiful daughter Nadia. A kind man who thrived on the success of his people, the love the pack had for their alpha was pure, with a fearless mate. Sky was a true warrior at heart. The morning star pack was full of proud wolves with many great strengths. Morning Star pack thrived.

Little did the royals know that the Silent Hunt and Blood curse alphas had a great disgust for their pure kind. The royals saw the werewolves as a blessing yet that was not mutual. Lycans began to be mated to the other clans and the were-wolves were banded from interference. Mating was to be sacred yet these clans began hiding their women in the woods and the building of underground bunkers began. Most had been abused in their trades.

All the clans Alpha's and Luna's were to attend the annual conference that takes place at a different clan each year to discuss laws, and exchanges for materials. This year was Blood Curses packs year to host. Alpha Augustus Sage and Luna Syvia sent their Beta in their place, rogue attacks threatening the clans safety and stayed to protect the pack. Alpha Bruin Maximus traveled to protect his ally along with his warriors with his pack.

Upon arrival the village was empty of all life. No children, no women or men. Just a eerie breeze. It was cold in the September air. The pack should have been busy with winter preparations. Dead silence and so sign of life. Their beasts on high alert.

The first blow was a silver spike threw king Lorances heart. Towers from 40 feet above hold wolves carrying on the assault and threw the trees the attack was vicious. Silver filled arrows flew in the evening sky like a colony of bats to the victims belong. No one was sparred. In the weakened state of the leaders and travel companions the wolves appeared from their posts onto the ground to tear the lycans apart.

While the murder was taking place the remaining unprotected clans were being burned, raped and eliminated in their homelands.

Night meadow was able to save Morning Star from the assault although the last remaining live from Celtic Beasts was the late kings son. Bruin was charged with raising him in his pack and protecting his identity. He must never speak of who he is or who's blood runs threw his veins so he may live long enough to carry on his legacy.

Alpha August Sage was crowned king and took in any that survived from all the packs, distributed amongst the surviving clans or move to other packs if they wish.

Zander and Wendell were sentenced to death for their attack. Their innocent pack members as well as Zanders son and mate were sparred and taken in by an American pack.

The clans began split off into packs Traveling away from the horror they suffered.

The king remaining in Ireland with hopes to someday send his heirs to America to expand once the clans heal.

The day that night meadows bravery became a bedtime story for kids.

The day Celtic Beast ceased to exist.

Chapter 3

S eptember 1989

Rupert Astrid

Nessie has been in labor for 12 hours. The sweat has coated her beautiful face in a thick glossy mask. It is almost time for the arrival of my heir and our beautiful child.

She is throwing threatening glares in all directions ready to strike. I want to sooth her pain but that is not a possibility. I direct my attention to the sight above me to ease my suffering.

We use a special room in the alpha hospital wing with a glass ceiling so our pups can be born under the power of the moon. An ancient ritual but a beautiful one in my eyes. The stars are a gorgeous site to see as the constellation Libra is in plain sight and the new moon although barely visible, my predator vision can see it perfectly.

I am confident that it has taken my mate this long to deliver, due to the nature of mine and my beautiful mates relationship stressing her body, I have loved her since I laid eyes on her. She was a Rouge traveler from the north. She was alone and traveled beyond our borders. Her dark auburn and brown hair straight down her back, Nessie was a thin woman and slender face held light brown eyes with flecks of yellow.

She was a voluptuous women but when she chose to stay she let herself go. Her skin was tan but muted by the cold. She was radiant with the snow fall. She made it very clear a lycan mate was not wanted by her. I gave her a home. Not my home since she did not want my love or affection but her own beside the castle in case she needed anything. I requested she stay at least so we didn't weaken from the bond.

Nessies heat hit after a few months of her staying, like a wave of hypnosis took over her mind as she broke down my bedroom door crazed with the heats demand and here we are. Bring a living miracle into this world and Nessie hates us all. Lycan pregnancies are shorter. Her being a pure Werewolf she carried for 9 months. The mother and her species determined the pregnancy length. The pup develops their lycan side at 2 years old were as the wolf side comes at 16. Nessie never gave our growing life a chance to see. All she sees in her dark mind is an abomination. Lycans are frowned upon in the pure Werewolf community, no one knows this side of me except my mate. Although hidden for safety purposes my mate literally could smell it.

"Nessie I will not force you to stay. I never have my dear but you must relax if you want this to end" I try to reason with her wolf. Eyes black as onix fixated on me.

"I will not to be weakened by this moon forsaken bond" she snarls threw her bared teeth. Vira her wolf very present and damn near feral.

It fades with a powerful contraction that makes her body shake, her scream makes me want to hold her but she never would allow that.

"Alpha she won't with you here" Thompson my Beta whispers in my ear.

"Alpha Astrid it's OK we can take it from here" Dr Diarra spoke firm but carefully to not to piss off my beast.

I nod and leave the room. Standing straight across from the door waiting for my heart to be born since it is obvious that my mate doesn't have one. I feel the sweat on my brow, anxiety is building rapidly. How can Nessie refuse me the first glimpse of my pup. I never once forced her. I made sure she had everything including the choice to leave. Yet she continues to hurt me.

Pissed off I storm to open the solid oak door cracking the frame, barging in to the sight of the tiniest child being born and pulled from between my mates legs with curly bleach blonde locks with a strip of red.

The first scream was magic and my big alpha aura melted away into a paranoid mess. Nessie starved herself to harm the baby and I feared for my child's health. The doctor took her to a table to be examined while a nurse checked on Nessie.

Felt like a lifetime and everything was so slow I barely registered the bed wheeling to my side.

"Monstrous mistake. You were never mine demon" Nessie screams as she is transported still in the hospital bed to another hospital room to be cleaned and fed.

I stop them on the way out, looking her in the face.

"You are permitted to live here but that pup will see no harm. Keep away my dear and go about your life" my voice waivers. No mate should have to feel this. Rejected and unloved.

She simply smirks as if that is what she wanted, I move aside allowing them to remove her.

"September 30th under the new moon, 12am. 17 inches long 5 lbs 5 oz. Strong and healthy, just a bit small" Dr Diarra announced with a grin. Wrapping the tiny life in a thin blanket she walks over to me, passes the bundle to me so gentle. Tears of sorrow from the hate from my mate and also happiness for the new love in my hands.Bright blue eyes just like mine, her nose is so small. Very tiny in general.

"Congratulations Alpha you have a daughter " Dr Diarra smiles.

Her name already in my mind. So proud of this beautiful girl already for surviving her mother's negligence.

"Remi-Rain Astrid " I say loudly, applause fills the room.

I pull her close to my chest with aloud declaration of claim "mine"

Chapter 4

2o years later

Remi

Beauty. The first descriptive word that comes to mind when I see the beautiful natural resource in front of me. Sitting on the water bank watching the water reflect the afternoon sky like a photograph copying the different shades of blue and yellow that paint the sky as the sun begins to fade. Natures masterpiece imprinted in my brain for safe keeping. The wind caressing my skin moving my white dress in the wind and the clean smell of the water to my nose. Churchill Ontario such a beautiful place. The humans have moved on from this place and left it during the times of the wars.

Getting lost in the smell and joy the water brings my soul I almost missed a familiar scent approaching. I smile wide. The June air travels the scent.

" I'm no pup dad. I can smell you" the words stumbling as I laugh

He jumps out of the treeline in his large cream and chocolate wolf form at one last failed attempt to make me jump, just adds to my laughter. He huffs and nudges my brown leather bag before staring me down with his intense alpha eyes. As I am searching my bag for some pants he can put on he runs and jumps in the liquid heaven then taking a long thirsty drink. My father's wolf Goliath is handome.

He runs back up the small slope to shake off right next the me causing me to gasp and laugh at his foolish act.Handing him the black sweat pants he begins his change. Not to his human form but the form we try so hard to conceal. His bone shatter and form until he is 8 feet tall and standing on 2 legs as the beast. Fully covered in thick fur and standing in his glorious lycan form.

" I have to stop training you so well my little fire"

To anyone else that voice would be haunting. Deep and an unearthly thing to hear at first. The sound of 3 beasts speaking in full harmony is almost demonic but to me it sounds like love and home.

" You have taught me well. Papa would be proud " I smile with one stray tear

"He would love who you have become and how strong you are my little ember" His pride showing threw.

The slight sorrow in his eyes vanishes as quick as it came. My grandfather/papa was a lycan from Ireland were all the lycans resided until they moved to Canada. Of course there are some spread out everywhere for the king,to be his eyes in case of an uprising.

My Papa met my grandmother/Nana as a rogue on this land. He was already of higher ranks so the king offered him land in exchange for being a watchful eye. Yes I am aware that Papa and Nana are human terms but my grandparents adopted the term when they visited overseas for a treaty meeting. I loved it.

My grandfather Alpha Noris passed when I was 7, the old Beta Drak Eros poisoned my grandmother Luna Eileen for being an unnatural pairing in his eyes. My grandfather withered away soon after. He adored me and made it well known.Lycan and werewolf mates were unheard of and highly disgusted the supernatural community. My own mother former Luna Nessie rejected my father when I was 4 officially although she never embraced the bond, she refused to have another hybrid child and hated me greatly. The pack believes she went mad, which is not wrong. She openly dragged me to the dungeon and tried to kill me with a sliver knife to my heart for being an abomination. I was saved by our Current Beta Thompson Long, Drak's son. That same day she rejected him, I bare a crescent shaped scar above my heart as a reminder. My father smothered me in his affection and never let my confidence or self worth waver due to an absent mother. Beta Thompson and his son Jacob are incredibly loyal wolves and trusted family.

Stuck in my thoughts my father snuck away to shift and change. In human form he is still a large man. 7 feet tall and built like a true beast in his skin even without the fur. Dark blue eyes that fade to light with a ring around the pups, that changes from gold to green. Those loving gates to his soul comes from my nana, then he passed down to me. As well as his very light freckles and bright blonde hair with a strands of gold and red. I am a carbon copy of him. The only thing me and that bitch that birthed me have in common is my slender nose and thick body.

Thick but also fit and strong. C48 chest and 18 jeans, still can beat some serious ass when needed. I think what throws people off the most about me is my piercing littered face. My Irish heritage taught me that in some clans it was a sign of strength. There is also my choice in body art. Celtic mixed with meaningful tattoos cover both arms, and thighs. On my right thigh reads "there's not much of my past self that I resonate with anymore, but I love her all the same. She was growing. she fought so hard to get me here." Lengthy but powerful considering what my mother did to me.

I snap out of my thought once again to see him approaching.

He sits next to me in deep thought and wraps me in a protective embrace. It is getting harder and harder to sneak in the shadows about what we are. My forms are deep red with black tipped hair, the undercoat was white and my lycan form is about 7 feet fall, large for a female but my human form is only 5'4.I have to shift at night only with my father by my side so he can help keep prying eyes away since Ember my wolf is an unusual color and she doesn't like the attention. The Beta has this knowledge but the rest have no clue. Us hybrids can use one scent if we choose. We smell of alpha blood instead of a mix of what we truly are.

The main focus was to train me for when the nightmare came and we would be hunted. Becoming a crazed rogue is no option and my grandfather found this land and built it himself. The great Alpha Noris was kind and gave a home to any wolf that needed it. Maybe we are curses of the beautiful moon but we belong here.

For now we just sit and enjoy this beautiful peace away from watching wolf eyes.

It is now pitch black. We spent the entire evening here. The only light is the stars and stunning milkyway. We talked about mates and how strong he would have to be just to handle my strong will. Yet with hiding my lycan scent it will be hard for him to identify me. I would rather never have a mate and feel the loss of being unwanted because of my red beast.

Interrupted conversation when my father got a mindlink, a connection between pack member. Grey moves across his blue irises like the morning fog on the water. His hand grips his chest as he grumbles deep in his chest cavity.

"What is happening?!" I question repeatedly

Deep in our one way conversation I smell a pack member approaching but not one I care for. Unsure of my feelings the confusing unease creep up my spine. My firey wolf shows teeth in my mind and is ready to pounce. My father stands up tall from his seated position. I crouch ready to pounce, watching the treeline. Out of the deep dark forest our best hunter and head warrior stalks out.

" Zaden Stiles why are you prowling the woods at this hour? You are not on patrol this evening. There is a situation in the village you must return"

Zaden stares back with such intensity it pisses Ember off, the lack of respect for his alpha is disgraceful. He has been after me for years. Flirting, grabbed my ass a few times and even publicly asked to mark me, my father forcefully put him back in place 2 years ago leaving a permanent reminder on his skin that is littered with scars. He is my age and got his role from his father that retired.

"Predators hunt in the night for the most worthy prizes" his smirk makes me nauseous. " Isn't that right Remi" He practically drools like a wolf with rabies.

Time slowed for a moment. The musky dirt scent of our warriors pushes threw the thick forest. All a with distain pure of their faces. The forest was filled by many.

Without a thought my father shifts into his beast on 2 legs with very little effort. Almost like a magic act so swift.

"Ember. I love you. Shift and protect Remi" He demands

Their angry eyes enlarged 10 fold, eyes glowing with various shapes and shades of gold and attacked. 100s of wolf's shift, the scene that was pure bliss is now is a mix of fur and blood of our strongest wolves dying at my father's feet. I see Zadens timber coat and lack of fur were his scars remain.

I try to stop the shift, the fire burning my bones tells me its too late. Kill or be killed. This pain was different and the burning was unbearable.

My skin burns, the pain in my body matches my fear and anger. The burning turns into a heat. Pain worst than a first shift intensifies so great tears threat to spill. What felt like a large amount of time of rithing agony now was a burst of energy. I am on 4 paws that I don't recognize. Surely I am melting with this excusiating heat. Power rushes threw my veins. A new rush of overwhelming pure energy, I look at my paws and see the ground burning around me.

I step back in confusion and hear a heart shattered scream.

Half our army is shredded into nothing on the ground and into the forest. Blood of our own soiled the earth and could never be a beautiful place again. I search for signs of life and find the scene that will forever be burned into my memory. My father lays lifeless. His strong lycan body covered in silver knives and needles with a silver that burns my airways. What was once his strong neck was now a bleeding hole. A dagger in his chest and Zaden standing over him. With my father's throat muscles in his teeth.Disbelief, replaced with anger as hot tears sear and sizzle my ablazed face.

I felt the power shift in my body as the new alpha of our pack. The 4 legs I stand on start to crack and my spine elongate. Standing on 2 legs to fight this disgrace of a wolf only to see the full sight of the destruction. My heart, my blood laying dead before me. The warriors come full force, my large clawed hand grabs a grey wolf by its scruff, in one swift motion ripping his head from his body with my teeth. I could feel control slipping away with each kill at me feet. Crushing spines, severed heads and the taste of blood from those sworn to protect us.

Countless bodies at my feet, I want more. I want them all to die in my jaws to taste the wolves who took my father from me. A fit of uncontrollable rage. I feel a sharp pain in my neck. I go to reach for it but another pain in my spine then back. Howling for my pack the rage begins to die. I am slowing, falling. I see my father. Still on the dirt. Tranquilizers I can smell them.

"Daddy I love you. I tried to be strong. Please come back to me."

The wolves creep closer.My 2 legs snap back faster then ever and I can feel 4. One blast of energy, the will to escape. I turn and run for the water. Dodging more needles with poison. The water steaming at the contact with my burning skin.

Just as I make it I feel the needle in my head. I sway and say my prayer to the goddess herself. The cold dark water swallow my grieving soul and body. I welcome the darkness as my last sorrowful thought passes.

my grieving soul and body. I welcome the darkness as my last sorrowful thought passes.

Chapter 5

----

og. I can feel and almost see a blurred grey fog behind my eyes, the smokey figure behind my eyelids lighten as my awareness returns. The mix of silver and heavy duty tranquilizers deep in my blood I can taste it. I don't hear Ember as I open my eyes with great discomfort.

"I am here Remi" Ember announces herself weakly. Her voice weak yet still so smooth and elegant.

Thank the goddess.

My senses are slowly coming back but not my strength. I open my eyes to see a cement ceiling and the stench of bleach and death. A painful cough bursts from my throat and gag on the atrocious odor. A faint prick from my arm makes me more aware and ember to become conscious. I look to my left to see a hospital bag hanging from a metal hook. I smell the silver tinted liquid draining down the tube into my skin.Silver IV bag.

Ember echoes in my head with such weakness but still vicious " rip it out" I hear the pissed off snarl.

I reach down my arm for the needle, it feels heavy and the ache down my body is slowing me.

Finally reach the very thing taking my strength and pull the supply line out. Mustering all the strength I have I push myself to move with much protest. I get on my elbows to sit up, the weight of my own body exhausts me. Hell even this thin yellowing sheet feels as if it can hold me down, the lethargy setting in deep. I breathe deep gathering my energy. The stench of blood wafts up my nostrils. It smells new and old. The stench of Zaden is mixed with mine. Yet something familiar.

"Alpha Remi"

The voice is strained but powerful loyalty vibrate in those words, I know who the voice belongs to and is straight ahead 8 feet away.

"Jacob"

He is hanging from the concrete ceiling by his wrists secured in silver chains, the awful odor of wolfsbane stings my senses although not toxic to me it definitely is to him.His dark brown hair is crusted with blood. Those deep brown eyes bore into my soul. His power has shifted, Beta Thompson is no longer with us on earth. Jacob is now my Beta and most trusted friend. The new found power radiates off his beat body.

"Remi-Rain I am so sorry" He almost cries out but holds back. I can tell he has the urge to comfort me.

He has always been a soft spot for me. He is kind and strong. Like a big brother. Zaden used to throw profanity around saying he wanted to bed me but the truth is he is family. Pains me to see him so broken.

" Beta, explain" I don't recognize my own voice. Dry and full of power. Ember is trying to heal us from this pain.

His wolf Roman comes forward with weak grey eyes. Acknowledging his new status.

" The warriors turned. They attacked the pack. All who were loyal to our alpha have been eliminated and bodies burned. I was taken down by heavy tranquilizers before I made it to the lake. I felt him die" his grief leaking into the thick stale air."Them both. I tried to stop it" He whispers reliving the memories of both our fathers ceasting to exist.

Jacob's eyes change back to brown. Roman is wounded and goes back to the den in his mind.

"How many traitors?" I try to concentrate to gather knowledge. I am the only alpha blood and need to act as such.

My Beta closes him eyes with a sigh"More than half the pack and 2 Rouge clans"

The need to find escape was imperative. Using what sight I have to search, we are in the castles cells. Made with silver bars and toxic mixes to weaken any creature not just us wolves. I take a breath but the breath sends pain down to my stomach, back and thighs. Hot sticky fluid soaking my privates and stings with pain. A pained sob leaves my cracked lips. I sit up abruptly in realization and rip the sheet off. Ember releases an unearthly sound in agony and red hot anger.

Deep red almost black blood slicken my thighs and legs. The filthy hospital gown clings to my body.

"Jake close your eyes "

Hesitantly he obeys.

I lift the gown to examine myself fully. My fingers touch the source of the ache. Instant stings and melting pain. The rage. The sorrow. My insides burn. Absolute pure emotion. Father is dead and so is my innocence.

"Beta. Who?" My vocals are not my own. My beast is overpowering.

He lifts his head from its hung position. Eyes black as the dead of night.

"Zaden " He growls deep in his chest

"How long ago beta" enraged. Growing impatient although not Jake's fault.

"2 weeks, then often after and again before you awoke"

Everything slows. The fear poisons my thoughts as a faint nudge in my lower waistline.Under all the foul shit in this cell I can smell them. I focus my hearing. I close my eyes as tears leak from my eyes as I look at my beaten beta. His eyes droop to my stomach and back to my face.

" I hear 3 heartbeats including yours Remi "

I hear them too. So small and weak.

Lycans are only pregnant for 4 months.

The fire inside me burns bright. Pure fury and disgusted in my own kind, in my own body. Before I can speak the smell of my violator hits me in the face. I hear him come down the hall into my sight. The scars more noticeable in the light.

He smirks his grotesque smile, staring into the eyes of my beast as she surfaces.

" You will die in the flames, melt the skin from your bones into the nothingness that you are Zaden " the words are no longer my own but those of my dark beast.

He drops his joyful expression.

" Remi is that anyway to speak to your alpha and father of those pups " Zaden glares his sinister stare.

"Not my fucking alpha" I speak so amused and smile

Stepping back from the bars he snaps his fingers, a wolf I went to school with stalks closer to him holding a long gun. A tranq gun.

"Ryan Anderson we went to school together! We were friends and I am your alpha!" I scream in a pitch that hurts my own ears.Jacob snarled loud and protective.

Ryan was a friend. Sparred with me and even shared some meals with me. I used to find his 6 foot frame and grey eyes handsome.

"Traitorous mutt! Rupert took you in from nothing! He gave you a home and fed you." Jacob loses control of his weakened wolf but the disrespect for his fallen alpha pushes him to the surface.

"Unnatural abomination " Ryan spits his venom words, retreating up the hall

Zaden laughs a cackling noise.

"Your only friend will watch me destroy and own you until there is nothing left." He looks at Jacob with distain.

" Poor Beta wants a taste of his bitch lycan too bad all he gets to do is watch. Not like you haven't done it before isn't that right Remi" zaden vomits his accusation.

We have had visitors from other packs and although my virginity was intact doesn't mean I haven't done and received my fair share of sexual activities, that gives him no right to forcefully take what I refused. He took what was mine and my mates. Not that I will survive this or be wanted anyways. I am ruined. A thunderous growl leaves Jake's lips. Defending his alpha.

A whistle sounds threw the air and Jacob whimpers.

"Stay strong Remi-Rain " He rushed out in an intoxicated trance

He was out cold hanging limp, chains digging his wrists.

"My pups will be hybrids. If you hate us so much why breed me! Taken my body and defiled it!" Pure hatred fill those spoken words

"No former alpha. These pups with have the power of a lycan but the body of a werewolf. I will breed you over and over until the end result is a more powerful weres without the tained lycan line, that is what the carefully measured silver is for. To weaken not to kill. Any pups who fail will meet their grandfather with the godess."

Deep in thought the raise of the gun went unnoticed until I felt the burn in my neck, then so many burning needles are in my skin. Fading from grey to a blotchy black.

"Not my alpha " I whisper one last time

Swallowed by the dark with a deafening growl.

Chapter 6

R^emi

4 months. 4 long agonizing months. The hospital bed was removed and I now lay lifeless on the floor. Sweat drips from my dirty misshapen face as the silver tranquilizers start to wear off. Ember is snarling in my mind to weak to break threw but here enough to slowly heal my wounds. Disgusted and shame fill me daily at my weakened state and lack of clothing. I am reduced to wearing a bra and boy shorts only. The tattered hospital blanket under my abdomen is the only comfort for my pups pushing against my skin.

My hair is a gruesome shade of rust and mud from the blood spilt from my body. A favorite activity of the guards. Tranq me and beat me before I pass out, on occasion grope my body. I take great pride in taking a few eyes out of their sockets with my claws, one guards ear and ripping a throat out when they think I am about unconscious. One unfortunate soul Virgil wears my teeth marks, his left eye is replaced with glass and half his face look like it went threw meat tenderizing.

Zaden visits often to beat me into submission, he wants my alpha status that I refuse to pass to his greedy hands. He could kill me for it, the reason why he doesn't is simple. He wants a Luna. His obsessed behavior is sickening. That sad excuse of a man and wolf antagonizes my Beta that is now so weak they have no need to chain him anymore. His faint heartbeats are slowly decreasing. Tears fill my eyes seeing his struggle to breathe.

"Jake?" I choke on my sob and hiccup.

My mind is breaking from sadness, with madness creeping in. I am basically feral in this oversized cage.

" I am still with you my alpha" He wheeze out and coughs. Sprawled out by the bars."As I will be to watch the pups grow" I could hear Roman surface long enough to voice his loyalty to my pups.

"And us with you Beta"

I couldn't help but smile and hold my enlarged stomach. Their heart beats irregular due to the toxins and beatings we have survived. The thought of rejecting them was powerful in the early stages of new life growing. Jacob was a big influence on my change of heart. It's not their fault. This life growing inside me was not just that pile of shit Zaden. They hold a piece of my Papa, my father and I.

Today the cramping has been brutal. Not knowing if my babies will be ok with all this pain I have been feeling.

I can feel the effects of the full moon taking over my body. I can feel the surge of pure love and energy only the moon can provide. We don't have to see it to feel it but oh goddess do I wish I could see the blessing in the sky.

Ember stirs agitated"They are arriving "

I sniff the air deeply and get the same smell of this cell. Dispare and silver tinted blood.

Rush of fluids soak the concrete beneath me followed by a white burning pain in my back and front. The liquid tinted with blood soaks my undergarments. Agonizing pain takes over every molecule of my body.

Jacob hears me struggling and forces his poor broken body to move towards me. Crawling and dragging his massive size to my corner of the cell.

"Remi take my hand" He soothes my nerves. Rubbing my aching hand and sits up strong despite his condition.

"They can't have my babies Jake" I blubber in hysterics, tears smother my broken face. Contractions wrack my body in waves.

"They can't tell if they are lycans until they are 2. Hon look at me" He is no longer my Beta but my sweet friend as he grabs my face in his Large hands to force eye contact in my crazed state.

"They need you Remi-Rain. Now focus alpha " He is alert and eyes shining so brightly.

A powerful urgency came over me. The pressure in my birthing canal was so great but I had to sit up. Jacob pushed himself to move with speed sitting behind me his shredded legs at my sides.

"Remi we have to remove the underwear." The embarrassed and urgent sound from his lips drag me to do it quickly. I lift my ass to take them off, sliding them down quickly feeling the liquid smudge down my legs. Taking a moment to feel the bulging in my entrance. I knew this would be fast but didn't think it would be this fast. I am not ready.

The pressure is too great the urge to push is so primal and raw. My brave strong Beta reaches down to pull my legs up towards my dirt stained chest for traction.

"You are the great beautiful Alpha Remi-Rain Astrid of Black Forrest Pack." He whispers in my ear. He knew my confidence was wavering with pain and fear."You are strong. You are capable. You are a bad ass bitch" Jacob Continues to sooth me and hype me up just like in training.

"You will survive this. Now fucking push!" He growls the vibration rumbles in my chest.

I bare down and push with all that I have. Massive pain fuels my body. A loud cry leaves my lips. I will endure this for my children. The torture, the pain. My body taking all this making it feel as if I am splitting in half.

"Keep going!" He howls louder

I breathe in so deep it hurts and push once more. A burning sensation fills my privates but I keep pushing. I stretch down to feel a head full of hair slide out of me. Slight relief fills me for a moment with one finally push for the shoulders, Jacob releases my legs I pull this tiny body to my chest. A warm, sticky, large body squirms and let's out a strong cry. Tears well up in my eyes.

A son. I have a son.

He looks just like me except he has the redish Irish instead of my blonde to his hair. That joy faded fast with a pulsing contraction that made me cry out. One big grunting and the placenta gushes out. I feel sick at the sight but know what I must do.I bite the cord with my canines and free my son of the blob. Jacob reaching around me to move the afterbirth without even flinching. I breathe heavily while memorizing my sons face.Seems like no time passed when a more painful pulse hit. I finish the next wave hits harder and I push. Jacob takes my son and places him safely on the ripped up hospital blanket next to him and pulls my legs up once more. I push with everything I have and cry at the razor like burning in my vagina.

"Alpha keep pushing. Gather up that strength! Push!"

Delivering twins naturally was unheard of. Especially alpha twins. The power they use during pregnancy makes it damn near impossible and can result in death. My strength was draining and exhaustion heavy on my eyes.

He pulls my legs and I give my biggest pressure filled push.

"Please Selena my moon goddess give me strength, don't let my pups grow up without me in this place" I cry and pray.

My hands on Jacob's around my legs I push. Yelling out anything that comes to mind and push with all my goddess given strength.

The next contraction I keep pushing. I feel for the head ready to grab my pup.. pissed at this pain and situation I bite my lip and bare down. The burning disappears faster than the last. My fingertips feel more hair then the last and in one quick motion slides into my hands. So little. The afterbirth oozes out with one last grunt comes out and the excruciating hurt was now an ache. I waste no time biting that terrible tasting cord. Looking down at the life in my hands for the first time.

Blonde. My daughter has long locks of pure golden blonde and is so much smaller than her brother. Her lashes touch her cheeks and she cries out. She is beautiful.

"September 19th 11:45am and 20th at 12am" a small female voice says from the hall.

I place my daughter next to her much larger brother and let out a beastly snarl. My teeth started to shift. My pups. My babies. These cells have weakened my body but strengthened my primal instincts.

The familiar sting of my skin hits me hard, and then again. I lean against Jacob in heavy exhaustion. He shakes in rage. He holds my face speaking frantically, I don't understand him. His warm frame wrapped around me.

"She just gave birth what the fuck is wrong with you!" He spoke with strength and fear.

The familiar wisp of the dart filled the air.

Silence and falling into each other as he cushions my fall backwards yet my body still in such horrible pain. Jake is out too. I feel rushed feet around me and my sight is failing me. They are taking them. I want to move. Please move.

"Male 8.5 pounds 23 inches long and female 6 pounds and 19 inches long"

My babies. They are mine Ember snaps.

I can't move

Pure black sheets take my vision.

Chapter 7

---

1 year and 3 weeks later

The light shines threw the cell from the hallway light. Late in the night all I can think is how how disgusting it must be to live in a pack that holds a broken woman and her children in a cage for almost 2 years. To be the filthy low scub that helped destroy my life for greed and lust.

Zaden has not successfully mounted me in a year, the sight of his naked body in my drunk state was grotesque and his penis size is probably why he is on a power trip. He tried to make me conceive after the twins several times, unconscious of course knowing I would remove his manhood if given a golden opportunity to do so. I am unsure as to why possibly he failed due to the build up of toxins in my body or simply a blessing. No pregnancy came and I can not say I am not thankful because I thank the goddess nightly.

Deep in my nightmarish thoughts standing at the bars just watching the light flicker, snapping back to the horror I am in.

The toxins in my body are useless, after so much use Jacob and I have built up a tolerance to the poison I will forever taste on my tongue. Our strength has returned full force. The guards only stop to give food and Zaden has been absent for 6 months. Rumor from passing wolves is he is trying to expand in the south. Although futile since he is no alpha, his absence is crucial for tonight while the pack slacks without him here. One female let slip there is a celebration at our pub so most if not all will be shit face drunk. The struggle is doing this in human form until we reach the lake. They will smell my lycan or my wolf scent if I shift, that is how the pack found out about us even after masking it yet again I am sure in our sleep it must have leaked out.

Being in this form also insures we don't lose communication with the twins. We blocked all members of the pack except each other but the pups don't have wolves yet. I tried rejecting the pack members from the pack and using my alpha command. That resulted in me taking a 4 day nap and getting beaten in front of my pups. Our plan is crazy but we must free us to provide for the twins.

Luckily we won't be doing this in our undergarments. An omega was demanded to give us clothing with the intention of covering our bodies from each other. The sick bastard thinks I would fuck my Beta in this cell with my children in here.

Baggy grey shirt and black yoga shorts cover my body now thin body and Jake has grey sweats and an oversized shirt. We have been stashing clothes away for months for this. The kids are in sweats and t-shirts as well as the hoodies we stashed. I miss clothes. I miss everything out of this cell. I am afraid of being too feral to have such things. For now all I can get my small family is freedom. 1 week before my little pups are 2 years old and now is the time.

"Our pups have never felt the grass on their feet " Ember says in a hushed tone.

The statement was truthful yet pissed me off to my core fueling the urgency I already felt.

I turn around feeling eyes on my back. The twins sitting on opposite sides of Jake on the filthy floor, looking at me with scared eyes. Well not my son, with my grandmother's green eyes and Papa's red hair, he has the look of pure boredom and irritation in his eyes as he rests his hand on his slightly round cheek, with a hint of mischief in his expression. Lycan pups are advanced. So he may be almost 2 but in his mind he is about 5 years old.

"Aleric, my handsome son. Why the face?" I say as sweetly as I can. He is strong willed and very open with his thoughts.

"Mama I want to go. Sissy is scared and uncle Jay is fidgeting"

I smirk at Jacob, who is side eyeing my son with deep brown eyes of disapproval with some over grown brown hair in his face. Keeping his large arm around my daughter. He is 6'7 So my tiny pup looks bite sized next to his large frame.

" sweet girl it'll all be OK soon. I promise Nora" I whisper gentle to my big blue eyed pup that is on the verge of tears. She is so little it breaks me to see.

I kneel down and stroke her soft blonde hair as she cries. Just over her shoulder all the evidence of our kidnapping on the floor and walls. Starring at the bloody almost 2 year old brown stain from their birth, among others from mine and Jake's abuse. I blink my own tears away traumatized yet relieved the kids never got the treatment, but fear can be just as painful.

"OK mama" she sobs.

It is time. The sound of drunken activities has moved farther away from the prison and no guards in sight.

Anxiety, fear and hope flood me like a tsunami, exilerating and suffocating all at once.

The time has arrived. Now is the time to break my babies out of this hell. Jacob is preparing the children and rehearsing what they need to do. This needs to be fast but dead silent. For 2 year olds that can be difficult. I have faith in all of us. My hope is keeping me moving and my faith in my little family and the goddess.

"What is your part in the plan kids?" Jake sternly repeats for the 3rd time in 15 minutes.

"Stay close, once we get to the door and we get picked up by you or mama our only job is to hang on for the swim and stay quiet!" Nora says with such a soft voice leaking with enthusiasm you would think she was a fairy. Her energy is a blessing from the moon.

" I won't let anyone hurt my mom uncle Jay " the vicious growl came from the tiny body of my son.

"Aleric, I won't let that happen. If you can't follow the plan I fear what could happen to you all. Bud please " my Beta pleads with the tiny spit fire. I almost chuckle but seriousness sets back in. One wrong move and we all die a horrible death or worse. The thought sends nausea to my stomach.

"To keep mom and sissy safe, I swear I will" the heavy sigh that follows almost a grumble.

He will make a fine mate some day.

Jacob puts the plan in motion. Stretching our aching limbs, we must be ready for anything.

"Alpha once we start there is no return" He was in beta mode. We are on a mission.

I nod in full understanding

We are in motion.. quick and quiet. Walking behind him putting a backpack on Jacob full of clothes and beginning the first stages.

He turns to look at me, his glowing eyes looking into my soul. Kisses my forehead. He will always be my family in this life or with the godess.

Taking a calming breath gave him a deep quick hug to sooth my nerves. Releasing with a nod. It's now or never.

We both put our hand on the door bars and pull with all our strength burning our hands and the smell in putrid our skin is cooking at a fast rate as the silver acts like acid. I am breathing like a pissed off bull, I can feel my nostrils flare. The skin is screaming but I can't stop. Not now.

Breaking a heavy thick sweat, the pain is causing our wolves to come out and I sigh welcoming the strength. The crack of the door hinges and lock mechanism snapping is exilerating.

Jacob takes the door from my mutilated hands placing it on the ground inside the cell. Steals a glance at my fleshy burnt hands and takes an old shirt, makes bandages for my hands. He nods and steps out of the cell, takes a sniff and a look. Waving for the kids to follow we start moving.

Obediently they stay close and quiet. Bare feet sticking to the floor makes an awful sound as grime stretches on our toes, luckily the guards are at the pack bar disobeying Zaden as planned. The walk is short, yet feels like miles and the nerves grow with each step. We reach the final corner, stopping so Jacob can take a cautious look. With a nod taking a right and there sits what we are looking for. The 6 stairs lead to a large landing that goes outside in my sight makes me smile for a moment. Climbing the stairs holding the kids hands. The landing is large and is able to hold us all, I push the kids further behind me.

Jake points for the kids to back up more before reaching for the knobbed handle snapping the handle and lock clean off.

The door opens to the air I have dreamt of for so long my wolf surfaces. I push her back fearful her scent will travel. I go to the kids pulling their hoods up and tighten the strings.

"No peeking and no sound" I order them.

Picking my daughter up to secure her for a fast paced travel. I breathe her rose scent for my anxiety.

Nora is on my front tucking her tiny head into my neck to calm her quaking body, Aleric copies the movement when Jake picks him up.

" I love you all. one last time what do you need to do" my voice cracks

They both say at the same time in complete sync"ssshhhh"

Up the last step and I was alive. Pine, birch and grass attack my senses. Freedom.

Our steps were quick but quiet as a hunting predator. I can taste the fear seeping into my chest, holding my girl to me in hopes she calms my pumping heart. Jake is ahead of us watching and looking for danger. My sweaty hands tucked under my daughter securing her, burn from the cell door, hissing for a split second.

No. I refuse to acknowledge my wounds until my pups are safe.

"You can do this. You're a bad ass bitch alpha " Roman's monotone voice rings in my head.

Threw the thick dense forest. Wild brush pulls my clothes ripping holes, thorn bushes stabbing my legs and soles of my feet.

"Strength. Push threw must save pups" Ember pumping me up

I pause. The bank so dead of life and the ground blackened, were my father lost his life is the place we must pass to save his child and grandchildren. Flashes of his giant beast laying bloody. I shake it off and move forward.

"Move Remi danger is near" Ember hisses in disapproval of my memory.

So close to the lake. Our ticket out is threw the water that used to give me joy, the other small island off shore holds boats to bring us the rest of the way and mask our scent. The air is chilled but we will do what we must.

I stop. It is eerily silent. I can smell filth and sense a presence.

10 feet ahead a rushing Jake speeds with my son. Dead stops to sniff the cool awful stench.

"Jacob!" The fear in my voice cracks my courage. No longer an alpha. Alpha replaced by a scared mother.

Out of the shadows a deep brown filthy wolf snarling with anger leaps onto my back and lands a paw onto Nora's head into the gravel with a crack. The side of her face smashes the rock, she squirms as I push to release her to escape.

"Save my daughter!" I managed while this rabid animal pushed me further into the ground. I push my head to the side for air to the sight of Jacob running to Nora. My chest pushed into the damp freezing sand.

Jake scoops Nora up swiftly. Quickly finding a spot to hide my babies. Running to the large Boulder pile next to the water into the rocks to hide them with the bag tossing mud on them to mask their sweet aroma with the bag. Rushing back to the wolf pinning me down. My Beta pounces hard and fast.

The weight of this monster and Jake is crushing my lungs from my back. His teeth assault my body and paw crushing my skull. Elbowing the wolf in the ribs, earns me a painful howl from the traitor, rolling to free myself gasping for air. I spot Aleric holding his sister tight in the rock bed. Nora. My beautiful girl wearing blood down her face from the fall and tears of terror.

I see red hot smoke cover my vision. Like watching the scene frozen.

Everything goes in slow motion. The only 2 people that love these pups could die right here and they are watching. The screams are desperate and crush my heart.

Hot. Sweating, burning heat expels from my body. My already burned hands are in pure agony. My bones crack and muscles ache. Stretching to release my beast. The heat becomes a comforting shield. My hands regenerating new skin before my eyes. The flames swirl out of my newly spouted fur spiking threw my pale skin as I stand in my lycan form.

Jacob is in a state of shock as he has never seen this form. I have never seen this burning hell hound that is my lycan.

The attacking wolf is frozen in his place in submission, my beast sees old blood and death. My fathers blood marks this land, my ancestors created this place were we meet an untimely demise. Never again. Wrapping my burning beasts elongated claws around his neck with intent to crush his airway. The flames spread all over his fur, synged fur falls from his throat. Melting hair and muscle fall from his body. Watching his light leave his body. One final gasp leaves his melted throat and goes limp.

I take in my surroundings. Everything is engulfed in the flames I produce from my beast. The forest is falling to ash, all that lives is dying in leaving the village below in perfect view to watch it all fall is a beautiful sight.

The night sky fills with the burning embers and smoke. Faint screams and hatred fill the air as I watch as the heart of my suffering burn in beautiful a shade that looks as stunning as morning glow. I inhale the chaos as if my life depends on it like the psychotic bitch they carved me to be. I will watch it all burn to protect my pup and purge this world.

My pups, I panic searching for my babies. Heart beating in my ears.Jake is in the water with both children in arms protecting them from my flames, shivering wide eyed in awe.I take a deep breath and contort my bones painfully. I am standing naked on the shoreline. My Beta stares for a moment before rushing to put the kids on their feet and give his alpha his shirt. Pulling the huge shirt over my head"Remi-Rain what in the actual fuck was that?!" His shock clear in his voice

"Shit. I don't know Jake! I am so fucking lost!"

He hugs me tight, shaking from this madness that destroyed my papa's land.

"Talk and process later. We have to swim" I nod in agreement. Taking off the shirt and Jacob tying the backpack to Nora. He copies my action with his pants out of the watchful eyes of the kids. Shifting quickly into wolf form. My wolf form is less scary.Aleric holding the shirt I wore tightly. Roman taking over transforms into Jake's cream and white wolf.

The kids settle in on our backs as we take the chilly swim to freedom.

Chapter 8

King Alpha Silas Evensen

Sitting in yet another long clans meeting. Since moving from, Ireland it seems all that is on my agenda are these meetings. Pure annoyance must be plastered on my unshaven face considering my wolf Abraxis is snarling in my mind, spit leaving his mouth. I inherited my father's yellow hazel eyes that are as bright as the fiery sun when my patience runs thin.

My parents stayed in Ireland while I moved most of our pack to America in the northeast kingdom. After not finding my mate I am determined to focus elsewhere. There are many that don't follow our rules here and that sure as hell is going to change.

I space out at the decor. The earth toned room matched most of the castle. Light green walls with chocolate brown accents mixed with some lighter variations. Bringing the colors of nature in my place of peace.

"Your highness?" My second in command snaps me out of my thoughts that he is instantly rewarded with a deep earth shaking growl.

Closing my eyes to breath away the rage my wolf unleashed. A few more moments is all I need. Abraxis knows who the fuck is in charge, he may sneak an outburst when we share emotions but I am King. Shaking out his deep burgundy fur retreats to my mental den.

" I apologize Beta Killian please continue in a faster manner. My beast and I have had enough of these meetings. " my voice loud and full of poison. This is the 6th meeting in 2 months. All the same shit.

"My son has a valid reason for irritation. Unless there is something new to discuss other than my last topic of choice this gathering is at it's end" the deep unnerving voice of my father spreads the tension.

Killian Blanch has been my best friend since childhood. He has grown into a large man, with his coal colored eyes, deep brown skin and braided black hair he definitely fits into our viking pack. My father went centuries without a Beta and our pack suffered for it. Being 25 years old without a mate was against us as it is, when I took the thrown from my father at 20 I knighted him as my Beta. Killian is loyal to a fault, on that same note he doesn't take my shit either and that is a quality I need with Abraxis being the feral unruly fucker he is.

"There was a reported massacre involving Black Forest Pack farther in the south about 90 miles from here, it seems that there are only 5 survivors your highness. One of the survivors is claiming he has been the alpha for a couple years but that means that Alpha Rupert Astrid and his daughter are deceased. Something is not right here Si." His eyes full of concern and fear for letting my name slip in front of other Alpha's.

Bowing his head in submission as an apology which I quickly accept. He has peaked my interest for sure almost in disbelief.

"Send a team of our finest warriors to investigate the pack and village. I don't want them to return until they search all that is left. Beta Killian and I will go threw the forest surroundings for more possible threats, survivors and evidence. Our most precious law has been broken" Abraxis was in a front row seat. We must never kill our own kind unless to defend someone who can not do so themselves or to protect your own life. Alpha's are known for killing for lack of respect as am I. This however was outright genocide of an entire pack.

"Father I request that you and mother remain on the throne, I will be gone for a few weeks. " graciously accepting my request with a stern nod. After what happened so long ago to our clans this is personal.

"One last agenda topic before we go to our quarters for the evening " My father said with a wariness I am unfamiliar with.

"On with it I am done with this shit" my growl heavy in ever word.

" Son I brought someone with me that I think you should meet" mindlinking his top guard.

A young woman enters the room. Her hair a deep earthy brown which you would think was black if you looked really fast, she looked at me with weary deep amber eyes. She was a thin build, not usually my type at all, given that I must say she is beautiful in her own way. She seems eager and uncomfortable all at once.

My father's shaking voice breaks the tension or at least a failed attempt "This is Angel Woods. She has graciously agreed to accompany us to meet you. She has been threw Luna training and I believe you both could help each other. "

I see black film coming to my vision. I don't need a mate. I gave up the need years ago and will not allow anyone to push some woman on me simply because they want me to get laid and have pups. I have fucked many women, dominated them fully and I can say the desire to fill the position of Luna was never a thought.

Holding Abraxis back with all my strength is a lose lose if I do not leave.

Walking to the mirror on the wall to inspect the damage to see my eyes are as black as deep ocean water under a night sky. Fixing my warrior braids before looking at the woman offered to me.

"Angel my Gamma will show you to your room which will not be mine. You can stay if you wish under my protection with the simple understanding that you will never be my Luna. " I turn to my father releasing a breathy snarl threw my protruding teeth.

"Killian we leave tonight. We have hunting to do" the his on my inner demons seeping into every soul in the room as I exit.

I need some fresh blood on my hands.

Chapter 9

R emi

4 weeks later

The twins birthday has come and gone. The signs of lycan genetics are unbearably strong, Aleric has grown 10 inches at least and his appetite is out of control. We passed threw one village as quickly as we could gathering supplies and getting my piercings redone so I could feel like myself again and the woman was happy to take some fresh herbs I picked in exchange in exchange.

"Every woman should express and be unapologetically themselves" the woman said to me. Gave me some much needed confidence.

The rest of the village wanted bigger compensation. The village was small and so mystical. Aleric in that 1.5 hour period ate 4 raw steaks from a stand and an entire bag of apples. We had to flee rather quickly before my growing boy stole anything else. Nora though her energy is depleting so fast and when she is awake she is fast moving, so fast she hurts herself at times. I knew lycan pups grew at a quick rate but my boy is almost the size of a 4 year old when he is only 2. Nora seems to be growing more in power since she is still so little.

Trying to teach them the lycan ways such as being descret and to control the urges was proven difficult while on the run. Staying alert and being parents, Jacob and I are purely exhausted.

I sit by the fire most nights and mourn the loss of everything I loved so deeply. My father, my pack, my home all taken and then burned by my unknown forces that live in my body.

Walk, hunt, and sleep is our entire day plus the daily training with the twins. I want a life for them. I want Jacob to be happy and rebuild his life, I want to create a home for my ever growing pups. Zaden surely is looking for us all, I will give my life if that means he never gets his claws into me again or taken my pups. We must keep moving to keep him from gaining on us. Working all day to move and all night to plan the next day. Tonight was different.

The peaceful tree cover opens to a breath taking water front. The water smoothing over the rocks in waves of liquid calm. Each wave brings the cool October air to my face, the smell of the icy chill brings tears of my soul to the surface and joy for our freedom. A tornado of emotions. In this moment I need to cherish this moment. Winter is coming fast, we need to make a plan for the coldest months. For now I will wipe my tears and remember this small gift of nature.

Pulling on the long sleeve I acquired from a nice young woman a few weeks ago. We may be wolves but my body has not healed as good as Jake's. He is in great shape as for myself I am still healing old wounds. The chilly air feels amazing even if I feel ill at times. We built a tolerance to the poison given in that hell, doesn't mean it didn't do damage. Once it is out of my system I will thrive.

Jacob sits next to me watching the evening sky. The moon creeping into my soul and warming my heart. I can feel the goddess giving me strength to be who I need to be. To protect my family. Leaning my head on Jacob's lap I invite the sleep celene is offering me. Soothing sounds of the heart beats of my small family lull me to sleep.

"Mama we are hungry and Nora tripped so aaalll the deer are gone!" My furious son bellows, making me jump onto my feet. From a dead restful sleep. His little hands flying around dramatically pacing the frosted ground obviously about to lose his shit. My pup red in the face, fist clenched pissed off.

"I didn't mean to Ieric I wanted to help JJ hunt" Nora cries making her mispronounce his name with a sobbing hiccup.

I scoop her up wiping her sorrowful tears away and squeezing her tight, tears soak my shoulder. Her heavy breaths slowing. I kneel down and reach for Aleric, his brow creast and deep red face flared comes forward into the embrace. Their scent wastes away any doubts I could have about the day. We would have to visit a village. We need food and my poor pups need out of these woods for a few hours. Both of their bodies sink to me releasing the weight of all the anger.

"We will be OK my babies. I know it is hard being out here cold and hungry but we do not hurt each other even feelings. You are right to feel all these big feelings. Just try to be kind" I sooth my children and feel the tension fall away.

"All packed up and ready to go" My Beta sneaks forward to not ruin this much needed moment announcing it is time for our departure. The beauty of this place I will forever remember as a safe place. I hope I can return one day when it is safe.

Scooping up my tiny pup and Jacob places Aleric on his back we start our uphill travel. Steep painful walk. The rocks are hard and so cold on my feet since we have not been able to aquire shoes with no money and not many willing to trade. The cuts on my feet pulling apart with each step. The entire hill was torture, pep talking myself the entire way. My pups need food, I am a badass alpha. I can do this.

Jacob has longer legs and feet made of the hardest stone, his trip was faster. The blessing of a man brought Aleric to the top and rushed 1/4 of the way down to pick me and Nora up.

"Remi when we get food you need to eat this time" the stern look made my wolf stir but I knew he was right. The malnutrition was taking my abilities away.

He placed Nora down and bridal style held me.

"It is soft here with grass and moss. It will be a bit cold, I need you both to listen, stay close and walk. Mama needs me to help her" I imagined a silent nod as we began to move. I rested so comfortably not realizing I was falling asleep warm and safe.

Chapter 10

S ilas

My best warriors have questioned the so called alpha of Black Forest Pack repeatedly. A month and 7 days. The frost is colder and winter is in the November air, we have been in this ash filled hell hole. I came here once as a small boy and I tell you this is not what was in my memory. Lush, vast land filled with spectacular green trees, bushes that grew the sweetest berries and the lake was the definition on peace. Alpha Rupert was the heart of this place.

Every living thing was now burned and reduced to nothing. The forest, buildings and pack erased. I knew Alpha Rupert he was a great Alpha and man. The story behind his death seems impossible.

My Beta questioned him for 2 days upon his return, he claims to have been traveling to help wolves that needed a pack. His explanation for his title was simply that the previous

Alpha took his own life because of the rejection of his mate, information unknown to him I met with him just 4 years ago. Rupert was a true alpha and a fierce leader, taking his own life doesn't seem possible especially the way he spoke about his only child who's name slips my mind. I never got to meet his child since we went for a hunt together and I believe she was training far from our location.

I am a rather intelligent man that takes great pride in serving justice. This situation has me mind fucked. Searching the surrounding woods for anything that could help us was a waste of time. By the time we arrived there were no scents. None that seemed fresh and whoever covered their tracks was intelligent themselves since knowledge of how to cover up all evidence of travel is a talent and trained skill.

Alpha Zaden could not have done this. I don't believe he caused the forest or pack fires simply because he is a fucking idiot and there is something strange here. The fact that he was not on the grounds when it all took place, doesn't change that he is an idiot and the tracks were carefully taken care of.

He requested our help finding his mate that he refused to name at first, eventually he called her Rainie and specifically said her scent is natural vanilla with faint rose. The pathetic man has been inviting rogues into the pack even with no pack to be apart of. I am unsure what is happening here, one thing I do know for certain is he is not innocent. What he is guilty of

I am unable to say but Abraxis goes insane when he smells his stench.

"Your highness Zaden is missing. We tried to question him 3 days ago and he declined. Upon a second attempt today he has disappeared." My top warrior tells me in a calm manner.

That mother fucker fleed. Only the guilty flee. Fuming at the lack of cooperation and disloyalty. Abraxis is coming out in full force. The painful snapping of my joints and tense muscles stretch to accommodate my demonic beasts size. Fur burning every pore of my tan skin. Falling to My knees with a growl so intense my men kneel in submission. My alpha aura suffocating my men. My wolf is in full control. To spare my men I must remove myself.

"Your highness we must search the south there is nothing here" Killian gasps for air "campsites were found traveling north"

GO! Abraxis snaps threw the link before bolting away from my wolves. I need to run this out.

I will have to expand my search to not only find Zaden but the arsonists. For now we hunt.

Chapter 11

Cold. Icy pain mixed with the burn of the wind on my face. Stalking threw the snow quickly assaulting the ground in thick balls.

The storm blinding our way in violent flurries so hard my eyes can not open, face frozen with fear. We could smell the winter coming, I failed to see how close it was and now we are paying the ultimate frosty price.

I stalk threw the frozen over hell in a simple tank top and leggings, Jacob in a t-shirt, jeans and his pride trudging into the monster storm. Wrapping my pups in all the clothes available shirts, extra pants, socks and all the long sleeved hoodies.

Nora clung to me so tight our shivers were in sync as well as our rapid heartbeats. Aleric was alert, scouting as far as his snow filled eyes could see. Jacob turns and starts walking my way. Wrapping himself around me. The heat radiates into my bare skin, Nora stopped shivering and relaxes against him

"Aleric is heavier but he is staying warm as am I. His wolf side is developing fast. Taking him will warm you and I'll warm her up" it was almost an order but I don't give a fuck my baby is freezing to death.

Swapping children quickly to avoid her anymore discomfort. As soon as my son wraps around me I feel relief and heat takes over my skin. I start to move once again a little more quickly and see that Nora is fast asleep on Jacob's chest. I smile for the first time in days seeing both of my children content for a moment.

Aleric pulls my face to his so fast it almost hurts forcing me to stop. Snow gathering on my head soaking me from the lack of movement.

"Mama I can smell" his eyes so wide in anger and a bit of fear

"Baby boy that's normal you are adjusting to this new power and" I stopped my sentence forgetting what I was even saying.

No. Not here. Not in this frozen shithole.

We are all stopped knee deep in hard damp snow. Jake's eyes meet mine with a threat to kill. An unspoken knowing, lowering the children to the ground.

"Aleric go to your sister and RUN!" I am in pure panic. My tough rugged son froze.

Before anyone could move I look to the left towards a familiar stench.

Bursting threw the dead forest in my direction. Zaden running in human form toward Aleric and I. Followed by others.

Without a thought I pushed my pup out of the way and took the full blow of his charge landing on my back in the deep snow.

Struggling under his large frame with my weak neglected body. Bucking him as hard as can, his body slamming back into mine crushing my ribs. My face jerks to the side with the first blow. The sting spreads with another hard hit. I can't see beyond the pile of snow caving in on me and glimpses of Zadens scared skin.

The assault stops and I feel his ice cold hand run up my body. Groping my breast and holding my throat. Digging my claws into his skin, attempting to release my airways. He leans his face to mine, licking my cheek.

"You are mine. Your body is mine, your freedom is mine to take. Those pups are mine" He hisses drooling on my face forcing a gag from me.

"Mine" Ember snaps awake from her slumber of healing.

Everything is hot. Remembering the feeling from the lake all those week's ago. The heat and pain is quickly replacing fast with emense power trickling threw my veins like a dynamite wick. His hands on my body start to stick to my skin with black smoke flowing from me. He retracts his hands and sits up quickly allowing me to bend my legs and push my feet off his waist launching him back, successfully freeing my body, quickly getting to my feet.

My clothes begin to fall from my body in ashes whisping in the unforgiving wind, leaving me naked in human form standing in front of him. Flames fill my left hand warmth and power comes from my body in waves. An unfamiliar cool sensation trickles like water down my right arm like a cold rain. Embracing the new coolness. Water gravitates around my right hand. Bubbling power rushes me letting out a banshee like scream.

I search for Jacob who is fighting off the bastards following this waste of wolf fur. 20 feet away Aleric is guarding Nora with power of his own filling the air and clumps of what looks like rocks floating around his bulky boy frame. My instincts are not my own but those of my beast, letting out another scream into the air.

Fire engulfing Zadens followers and wind pulling them off the ground. Flames burning alive the levitating wolves, clothes mold to their skin. The smell of flesh attack my senses watching them writhe in pain in the winter air. Jacob runs to the kids watching me in awe and confusion.

We will reunite. Zanders turn. I turn to face my tormentor and joy spreads to see his afraid expression. I can smell his fear and it is satisfying. My beast still in control lifts her hands. I don't know how I know what to do, I have no control.

Zadens wide eyes start to water and panicked gasps for air can be easily heard as fluid rises up his throat. A mix of blood and other liquid pour from his mouth and nasal cavity. Rolling on the grounds to find relief that he will not get. Looks like a dam letting loose. The trees have caught on fire. Mixing with the smell of suffering.

His eyes are bulging. Content with this view of him. The heat and power turning back into the cold storm air. The fire and water disappear leaving me shivering from my lack of clothes. Zaden takes a large fluid filled breath.

Sniffing the air not recognizing the strong mint and pine smell coming threw the trees along with the others that are mixed together. Someone of high rank comes into view. I try to concentrate on the large dark man in front of me, black thick braids trail down his shoulders. I squat in the snow to cover my body from the eyes around me.

"I am Beta Killian Blanch of the royal pack or as you may know the kings clan, I mean no harm but we are instructed by our king to bring Alpha Zaden Stiles and the arsonist to the castle. Looks to me both are present."Killian spoke with power and respect.

He continues "You have traveled from Churchill to Vermont I must say I am impressed " with a small chuckle at the end

I am so exhausted and the need to get my small family out of this hell was great. Jacob is running to me kids in his large arms. I hear him whisper to the kids to keep quiet. Which from their expressions wont be an issue since I am sure they are traumatized.

My teeth chatter now that the heat of my wolf is gone. Ember is in a deep sleep in the far corner of my mind. Killian stalks to my crouched form, Jacob let's out a breathy growl.

"I mean her no harm wolf. Let me help you get this woman and pups out of this cold. I can smell you are not mates but I still want to help with your family." Killian spoke with authority.

I nodded at Jacob and turned my eyes to the dark stranger.

" No one touches my children but Jacob as my ribs are broken. We will go willingly with the understanding that I want to bathe, feed and stay with my family" I demanded

"Understood " He agrees and snaps his fingers.

A group of men came forward handing me a thick blanket to wrap in, boots for Jacob and wrapping the kids up tight before returning to Jacob's arms.

I stood and fell right back down to my sitting position. The pain was awful but the exhaustion was worse.

Beta Killian lowers his body to be eye level with me so slowly. His smile is so kind and gentle.

"May I?" His voice almost a whisper.

I nod and shift my arms to hold the blanket as he lifts my broken body into his arms. Jacob holding both kids snuggled in close walking behind.

I don't know what will happen, one thing for sure is I get to bathe my children, feed and tuck them in like they deserve.

Under the protection of The last royal pack.

Watching Zaden be dragged behind lifeless was oh so satisfying.

Chapter 12

S ilas

I traveled as fast as possible back home. Receiving the call that both the fraudulent alpha and the pyro were both held in my clans land. I was proud of my beta for the capture of all the involved parties yet awaiting the rest of the information, Killian strongly advised that I gain the rest of the knowledge in person. Taking in a long breath absorbing the burned forest scene I stopped to see on my way home, where they were found was a large burned out fire pit. How this woman is able to cause so much destruction is beyond me.

Snapping out of my thoughts to focus on what is in front of me.

Travelling on foot threw the modern yet Victorian clans land. Houses of various antique colors and stained glass windows. Large snow covered lawns for children. Guards respectfully greeting clans members and keeping them safe.

I could have drove, but seeing my hard work and the peaceful life that we have built brings me and my wolf peace.

I nod and wave to my people. My wolves that I claim with pride. We are greatful for so many loyal souls. They make all this possible.

30 minutes is what it takes to get to my home on foot.

Reaching the silver laced gates of home they open to let me in.

This place is spectacular. The gates surround the entire building and two other separate buildings. silver laced but skillfully covered with beautiful hedges and vines. Stretching 60 feet away from the building to keep the effects from reaching our senses. The compound consists of the cells which are underground as you enter many yards from my home, the guest house just before the main building on the right and then the royal pack house. I could smell the false alpha as I pass the cells entrance.

Up the stone walkway the statue of a wolf curled up sleeping with her mate wrapped around. The water frozen in the pool underneath.

Just beyond the 3 story massive building stands in its glory. Brown marble with white granite trim with wild rose vines. During the warm months it is remarkable. The guest home is a modern wood cabin. To give the feel of the woods, I escape there at times with it being so far from the house and close at the same time. Quiet.

I smell something is off when I pass the guest home, Abraxis is on alert. I take a big breath in taking in the scent. Vanilla? I continue knowing my security has all threats detained. I did notice 20 guards around the building which was odd. I need debriefing like now.

Walking up the white marble steps and threw the giant maple door. Heavy footed from my long journey.

" Alpha so good to have you home." Killian greeted me with a hug and a slap on the back which I returned.

" I am exhausted so let's get right to it. What is Zadens current state?" My need for information obviously showing.

"Stiles will not give information other than accusing us of holding his mate from him and threatening an uprising" Killian was void of all emotions.   Making it clear that this situation is wearing on his patience. Which says a lot since he has the patience of a saint.

" We will bring him and his mate for questioning after I have a shower. What about the female what is her condition?"

My beta went silent. Head down.

" She refused to give any information alpha. There is a couple complications we need to speak about." Killian was choosing his words carefully.

" She is in the guest house with a few others. I could smell them on my way in. I simply need to know why? Why not the cells?" I questioned the smell on the way in. I trust my beta have an appropriate answer.

"The female has 2 lycan children with her and a male. Not her mate, seems to be her protector. She won't tell us anything but she requested to feed, bathe and tuck in her kids when she got here nothing more" Killian spoke strong about this.

I absorbed the information. This woman and man walked from Canada to Vermont on foot? With 2 children?

I walked passed him to the grand staircase.

" Alpha?"

I turn back to face my beta.

" Bring them plenty of food, clothing and make sure them kids have everything they need. We will meet in the thrown room at 7:30 after the children are asleep. She will need to be cuffed but explain that it is just a formality" I turn to continue to my destination. A shower is much needed.

Chapter 13

Remi

It has been a few days since I woke up in this strange place. I knew we were under surveillance and couldn't leave. After a few days of being able to feed my pups, bathe them and cuddle them close in a bed, I am just soaking up the normalcy. The browns and greens of the forest inside makes this feel like a home but I couldn't afford to get comfortable.

Jacob sleeps in front of the door most nights while I sleep at the foot of the twins bed. Jolting awake nightly at the terrors that haunt my mind, if it's not me it's one of the twins and once Jake too.

The alpha king wants to meet with Jake and I after the twins are in bed. Nerves are choking me but I know I must be as respectful as possible. Being held captive has made me more beast and I am hoping it doesn't cause our deaths.

I walk into the massive bathroom, the walls are murals of a vast forest. The leaves are gold and red, a full fall scene so miraculous. I strip my clothes for the first time in days, afraid to leave my pups and Jacob. My once gold hair and blue eyes tainted with filth and sorrow.

A stray tear leaves a white trail on my dirty cheeks. I walk on the cold wood floor to a hot much needed bath in the most powerful and wonderful smelling vanilla bubbles. I step inside and sink. All the dirt falls away as I scrub. The bite mark scar on my left side has never faded and faint stretch marks from my pregnancy.

I scrub them as if my life depends on it. Washing everything away. Every trace of my pain. I will rise again but first I must wash away the ashes of my past.

Both of the kids were out cold by 7pm. They have been sleeping so good aside from the nightmares. They look peaceful. Quietly walking to the king size bed they are snuggled tight into. Kissing their heads softly. Alerics fresh rain and spruce scent almost over powers Nora's sweet Lilly vanilla scent. I inhale deeply remembering their clean and clear aromas before going to the bathroom to get ready. Reminding Ember to help me keep my lycan scent scent covered. I know they are lycans here but I don't feel safe enough to show them who I am just yet.

I was given a bag of clothes and some make up earlier from a nice woman named Ella. She was so kind and very beautiful with her deep brown hair with undertones of auburn and her eyes looked like honey in the sunlight.

It has been so long since I used make up so I did something light to not overwhelm myself. I used light brown in my crease and light nude on my lid with some mascara. There's a pretty nude brown I used on my lips. They gave me a gorgeous mauve long tank top fitted that fit my curves or what was left of them and dark chocolate brown leggings.

I thought it would be more formal but the attire was very casual.

I stand waiting for further orders in the deep green sitting room with tan and cream furniture, Jacob walks in with his face clean shaved and wearing all black. Hair slicked back and looking more like himself, before we were held captive.

"Don't you look nice" he smiles at me.

"As do you beta Jacob" I say almost sarcastic.

The door opens to outside, a man dressed in a dark brown suit and tie steps inside. He is tallish for a lycan. 5'10 or so with light brown skin and almost black eyes which I am sure are brown most of the time.

"A pack doctor and nanny will watch over the children in your absence, they will not step foot inside unless needed. Please hold your hands out for restraints and come with me to the thrown room" in a monotone voice.

We knew this was coming, stepping out of the house into the blizzard outside. We did not resist.

They burned a little but we are used to it. Starting our walk to the enormous building ahead.

" I am Gamma Nicholas Visar, please remember you are on Royal grounds, you are safe but respect is expected at all times especially to the king. Follow me."

What the fuck kind of mess are we in now?

Chapter 14

Silas

Sitting in the throne room. Looking at the fine details of this room, my mother Luna Ella Evensen was the inspiration for this amazing part of the mansion. My mother's favorite season is autumn. Reds, yellows and oranges create a masterpiece. The floor is a fall forest scene much like the guest house bathroom. This room is large enough to hold 3500 people if you count the 2 balcony floors above and the balcony to outside.

Straight ahead a set of intricate gold double doors laced in green painted ivy along the frame. The handles are skillfully cut and carved red roses. My eyes wander to the matching set to my right. Watching waiting to meet this mute girl.

"We have been here for an hour. I can smell her here, this has been a huge misunderstanding please your highness give me my mate. I told you all that I know" Zaden pleading for what seems like the 100th time. My attention snaps back to this pile of shit.

A very beaten Zaden sits in the center of the room. Scabs forming around his open wounds. The fuckin idiot attempted to take out 10 of my warriors. Injured one unfortunately, but Zaden got his ass beat before the injured wolf would see a doctor.

I smile at his broken state. Pride fills me at the thought. My warriors are strong even while injured.

His story is far fetched. His side of what has happened is unclear and surely can't be honest. Alpha Rupert committed suicide. His so-called mate is here yet won't tell us her name and that her traveling partner assisted her in stealing his pups. The incident in the woods 10 miles from here is so confusing and an obvious cover up was his last chance.

The female and friend will be here soon, with any hope she will clear the air with some actual facts. This man in front of me sounds like an obsessed boy and is unhinged in so many ways.My demon is surfacing and Abraxis is loving the feeling.

"The female will tell us" my voice boomed threw the grand room.

"You can't trust her words! She has been poisoned!" Zaden screams.

Before I can put him in his place my Gamma Nicholas opens the side entrance. Making eye contact I nod him to continue.

First entered the male for about 20 paces. Built to take down a grizzly bear in human form. His attire surprised me, full black uniform is usually meant for beta status. I could smell he is of higher ranking which confuses me further. He faces me bowing his head in respect. For what was described as a feral animal he is what seems to be a respectful wolf.

Stopping dead in his tracks as he is about to kneel. Tilting his head back taking a long intake of air, no doubt smelling the stench in the room before turning his body towards the source.

The male looks forward towards Zaden. Making eye contact with the pathetic wolf and his eyes go from pure hatred to fear in less than a second spinning around to the door he entered.

" Your highness remove my bonds!" He ordered pissing my wolf off for a moment. I nod a quick response. I will deal with this issue later. I could subdue him if necessary.

Before we could release him he snapped his chains. I am the only one that has ever been able to break silver chains.

Running towards where he came as if his life depends on it, ready for an attack.

"Remi no!" The male yelled with all his power.

He colided with a very short figure. Flurries of blonde hair and arms pushing the male away. Before I could intervene in this insane match for power the male drops to his knees still holding the small figure that I can obviously see is the female. A feral deep haunting growl vibrates the room leaving me speechless. My nose is in overdrive. I can feel something. Something deep and hidden but now is not the time for this.

"Enough! Female speak!" Letting my king aura out just enough to get control of the room.

His arms wrapped tight around her chest and arms securing her. Long blonde red streaked hair hangs as her head is tilted down to her knees breathing heavy and chest is heaving. Even with her stretched clothes and messy hair in her face, she was stunning.

Taking a breath of a faint phenomenal scent, but not over powering. The aroma is being suppressed. Shaking my thoughts away feeling like a crazed wolf.

I stood from my Golden seat with hopes it would stop the situation from escalating further.

"Yes Remi babe that is quite enough. Feral bitch are you in heat? I could fix that. Do you want your Alpha to fix it?" Zaden laughs out in full belly laughing fit. I mindlinked my warriors to remove him.

Looking back to the restrained girl. Slightly moving her head side to side as if to relieve tension. Snapping her head upright, hair dangling wildly in front of her face.

Those eyes. The bluest shade, sapphire and gold. Her features are stunning and well defined. Jewelry glitters her nose, lips and eye brow.

Snapping out of my admiration with the most unearthly growl cutting threw the air like a knife. Her left eye turning the deepest red I have ever seen. Her body begins to smoke and what seems to be flames ignite and dance on her skin.

The male speaking softly to her. I don't think she is listening. Squeezing her tighter hanging on for dear life.He screams in pain releasing her throwing his shirt that was now engulfed in fire. She stands walking so calmly as her clothes begin to disintegrate.

The room is shaking violently. Wind thrashing off the walls destroying the paint and smashing the windows. It is raining inside?

I look up to water falling from the ceiling drowning the floor and all of us with it, the male stuck in place by an invisible force as well as everyone in the room except me.

" You are a murderer! You are a pathetic wolf! You are a fucking disgrace! You are not my Alpha!" I can hear her beast losing control. Mascara streaming down her pale face.

"You are Zaden Stiles the worthless fraud " she continues.

I jumped down the steps and ran as fast as I could. Trying to steady my steps trudging threw the water shin deep and merciless wind. I must stop this. The elements pushing me to use all of my strength.

The sounds that fall from her lips are pure pain and power. Standing in her melting bra and leggings. Battling the elements with all my strength and speed.

I reach her and wrap her in my arms tight to stop this assault. Her chest pressing against mine, her pulse rapid. Waiting for the struggle and burn from her skin that never came. This slight calming sensation fills me, I expected heat but nothing but calm.

Like watching a camp fire burn out the flames disappear and all there is, is us. The water stops falling. She looks up at me with orange eyes lighter than the red before.

Abraxis howling in my mind. So unsure of what this must be.

She whispers so softly with flickering tired eyes going dead weight.

"I am Ember."

Chapter 15

R^{emi}

Darkness. That is all that I see. No emotions. No feeling. Simply floating in pure and quiet darkness. Such a beautiful feeling or lack there of. Soaking in this moment to myself.

I seem to be slowly sinking down to whatever is at the bottom of this black bliss. Air moving my limbs freely.

A hard surface pushes against my back assuming my dark travel has come to an end, allowing my body to move to a seated position to try to figure out what this place must be.

Light blinds my vision and I cover my eyes peeking slowly to let myself adjust to the new blinding light. The first thing I see is green and feel the cold wet grass on the souls of my feet, soaking my clothes.

Inspecting my body thoroughly for damage but there is none on my body that is now covered in a long flowy light grey dress with silky thin straps.

Investigating my surroundings further using my sight and smell. The view is vast thick forest, vibrant greens blur together in the fog. My eyes still adjusting to the brightness barely sees the figure stalking my way.

Out of the fog a massive pure red wolf the size of a grown buffalo walks in big steps my direction. I reach my hand out as if holding a gift, before I could go the rest of the way the large animal rested her oversized head on my palm. Yet I still feel calm not afraid. Her scent sending peace into my being.

" Hello Remi-Rain" the voice rang in my head. So sleek and feminine. A voice that could sooth any wolves broken heart.

I teared up. I could feel so much love through whatever this bond is. Pure and reminding me of my dad in a way.

I have no words.

"I have so little time and much information sweet Remi. I am Autumn" The wolf pushed her word into my mind. I nod in understanding.

"You are special. You are developing your newfound powers, bound as a pup for protection. The binding was undone when your father gave his life protecting you. When you awake this information will guide you to more outside of this realm. The spirit realm."

I stop myself from asking any questions and wait for more. My father always taught me listening is more skillful than speaking. Too many questions too early can complicate things.

"You have been gifted with many instead of one, gifts from the blood we share with an extra from your ancestors." I smile at her words.

I have heard of visits from shared bloodlines but never did I think I would even meet one of mine. Not knowing my full heritage.

"My time has run out my beautiful Remi. You share these gifts with all who you are bound to. Try to remember" Taking a deep breath flaring her snout.

"Celtic Beast Clan lives in your veins. We all love you."

In an instant everything is black once again and I am falling. Not slow like before. My body is thrashing in the dark air. Screaming without a sound leaving my mouth drying the saliva causing me to choke.

Hitting the cold, hard ground with my face and chest so hard the air in my lungs escapes. Rolling onto my back painfully coming face to face with Zaden.

I sit up fast just to be slammed back down. Frantically moving I realize I am strapped down on the concrete floor. I hear his shoes walking next to my body rather fast. Straddling my waist and grabbing my face.

"They are mine" he spits in my face with every word. His eyes wander to my body." And so is this" slowly running his hand down my thrashing body.

The room is filled with light slowly engulfing the room. I scream profanity begging for help.

His weight leaves my body, the room disappears and in a second I am jerking upright in a bed. Screaming at the top of my lungs.

Many eyes are on me with surprised and fearful glares.

I jump off the large bed running towards the corner of the room.

" Get the fuck away from me!" My words sound more like a frightened child.

The snarls leaving my lips are wild.

Every wolf in the room stopped to stare. Where the hell am I? Why are these people here?

" Where are my fucking pups?!" Growling every word. Am I scared? Pissed?

All I know for sure is I know no one in this room. Nothing is familiar, my beta and pups are not here. Am I a prisoner?

Taking the moment to assess the people around me and the bright white room. Medical supplies neatly sitting on tables along the walls. It smells clean but not of a hospital. I take this time to look out the window with bars to see I am three stories from the ground. I must be in the main house still, the fountain is out front. I can see the house we left earlier today.

"I'm coming babies" I say to myself out loud.

I wrap my hands tightly around the thick bars ripping then clean off with very little effort throwing the bars into the glass, shards of glass fall to the ground.

I look out the hole I made. My escape. Ember coming to my mind letting her maturnal instincts take over my body and whispers so softly.

" Jump"

Chapter 16

S ilas

    I pace my office waiting for news on the female I now know her name is Remi-Rain. "Such a unique name." Abraxis adds to my thoughts.

No I must focus. After what had happened in the thrown room I sent the male to receive medical treatment and back to the pups for now. My parents and Killian are included in this conversation since I am completely mind fucked.

She is currently in a spare room receiving medical care on the third floor. The pack hospital would ask questions we can not answer for the time being. We have been silent in this room for a few hours thinking and simply just processing the events of today

"That woman was on fire!" Killian yelled letting some of what he has held back for hours out.

We are all in shock for obvious reasons.

My mother makes eye contact with me and smiles wide at me. How can this woman smile at a time like this beyond me.

"My son I think we must have a conversation about some history that may enlighten us all." My mother interrupted my confused thoughts.

"Mother as much as I would love to hear about our great history now is simply not the time. That girl all but destroyed the throne room as well as some scattered damage."

I feel bad for snapping at the woman who gave me life, but I don't need a fuckin history lesson. That female is a creature I have never seen. I have a demonic entity living inside me so I know all about odd family history and still can't figure out what happened.

"Silas Evensen king or not you will listen to your mother! She has information now sit your ass down and listen!" Slamming his fist on my table cracking the wood. My father's demon is out to play and he is pissed.

My wolf not taking kindly to his title being pushed snaps.

"I will respectfully hear out my mother but do not forget where you are father this is my clan" Abraxis and my demon become one to deliver this message.

The tension in the air is so thick you could take a bite out of it.

Mother clearing her throat to get the attention of the room. Looking me right in the eyes, sending me love in silence.

"Surely you know that our family was crowned after the great clans battle, we were sure that the Celtic Beast clans bloodline had died out and become extinct or at the very least their royal abilities since one of their children survived but no abilities were recorded. Our clan inherited the demonic entity that lives along side our wolves. The original royal clan got other abilities. We thought they had been bred out and lost track of the line and assumed as I stated before that the line was dead" She pauses to make sure we are all following and understand.

We simultaneously nod for her to continue.

"What has not been passed down in stories over time were their gifts. We all know they are the original royal line, none know of the elemental abilities they used to possess. Earth, air, fire and water. One gift per wolf or at least that was the story your grandmother told me." Tears well in her eyes as she tells us this bedtime story or from what I hear reality.

"The female has all the elemental gifts. Remi is the lost bloodline she has to be." She ends her sentence in joyful tears. Our original king and queen live on in this girl.

Sitting in the throne room taking in all the damage. I have already got the plans rolling to fix all that is broken. My mind wandering to the few seconds I held her close making eye contact with those fire filled eyes.

"I want to see her again I must know what she is hiding." Abraxis declared.

"We must question her first. The situation is not handled and I must understand our connection. She is suppressing her aura and lycan side still " he snarls at me before coming forward on alert.

Not understanding why he stopped arguing. Our alertness becomes one hearing running on the grand staircase. Standing and sprinting to the action just outside the room. Meeting my Gamma at the bottom of the stairs.

" She jumped your highness she is fleeing to the guest house" Nicholas informing me before running out the front door.

Hot on his heels the run was short. I waste no time busting in the door. The female stands in a protective manner in front of the male holding both crying pups in the sitting area.

"Remi it is ok! I won't let them take them!" The male trying to calm the wild woman.

"You can't take them! Zaden can not have my pups!" She was ready to attack at any moment.

"Female we need to speak with you! Surrender to your Alpha!" Power radiating from my every word.

"Not my fucking Alpha!" She screeches and the house shakes.

Running full force towards me and just as she pushes me back a flicker in my mind takes over my vision. Like a projected movie with smell and touch. Watching from a point of view that is not my own. A visual minklink of sorts.

Watching who I know to be Alpha Rupert laying in the dirt missing his throat. As quickly as the image came another replaced it. Smell of chemicals and decomposing bodies reaching a hand down to feel blood. Images of being stabbed, beaten and starved come and go so fast. So quick I feel my stomach churn. Then it all stops on one image.

Zaden comes into view. His hand sliding down on this naked body. Struggling to breathe and the taste of silver disappears.

Laying on a cold floor with the male close watching people come in and out of what I think is a cell. Taking two small pups as my eyes shut.

The scene is flashes of flames, running holding the pups, the freezing snow and then the clearing. Zaden drowning in his fluids and the trees on fire. Killian wrapping a blanket and smiling.

Her memories. This has to be her memories. I feel tears, as an Alpha I do not show weakness yet this slide show has me pouring my soul out.

The memory melting away. The house is back and I am on my knees. The male and female in front of me. She takes a step in my direction. This girl is fierce, a spitfire for sure.

"My name's is not female. My name is Remi-Rain. Alpha Remi-Rain Astrid."

Chapter 17

R emi

Two weeks. Two long ass weeks in this house. King Silas Evensen stormed out and I have not seen anyone aside from a few omegas bringing us clean clothes and food. Nicholas stopped in this morning to speak to Jacob about a private meeting with just him.

Jacob has gone with him I am assuming for questioning.

I stand here worried about his safety in this strange place. Attempting to ease my mind I check on my children. My pups whisper to one another on the bedroom floor. These children don't know how to play, I have tried many times with no success. They talk quietly to each other and to us, but no signs of play or laughter leave their lips.

Tears threaten to fall, I might be executed for my actions. Before I am called home to the goddess I need to see that my babies are happy. I know Jacob will take care of them but it's not the same as seeing it myself.

The sound of footsteps pull me to reality, I make my way to the dining room table that Jacob now sits at holding his head in his hands.

"Jacob" his name almost a whisper. Afraid of the outcome of the private meeting.

He looks up to face me. Obviously afraid of what my reaction will be to the information he has for me.

"They want the children to see a doctor in the pack house with only me. If that is successful the king wants to meet with us later." Keeping a calm tone

Anxiety sinks into my gut. Why do they want my children? Is this Zaden behind the scenes?

"Remi don't let your mind go wild Zaden is in a maximum security prison off the clans land, they just want to check the health of the kids and I believe it is safe for them." Jacob is so sure of his words yet cautious to not cause another outburst which we still know nothing about.

"I trust you Jake. I am in no position to argue and even so they need a check up. They don't leave your sight." Authority booms in my voice.

I have been listening to construction in the main building for 2 weeks after my wild outburst. It is no mystery as to why they don't want me back up in that room or even the building.

"Yes Alpha" confirming my orders.

Tiny footsteps that I know belong to my tiny girl sneaking behind me. I turn and crouch to meet her blue orbs.

"Mommy is it safe. To go see the new people" Nora's sweet soft voice.

"My girl, Jacob and I are certain it is safe. Aleric will be with you too. We would never chance your safety. Our love for you is too great to guess on something so big" My voice confident hoping to sooth her fear.

" I trust you mommy and uncle Jake." Nora whispers snuggling into my open arms.

"We can do this sissy, we can be brave like mommy and uncle Jake" Aleric comes behind her hugging us both tight.

I will burn this memory into my mind. Some day this will replace my pain.

Gamma Nicholas came to collect Jake and the kids about 30 minutes ago. Not before a lengthy conversation with Aleric about manners. That boy has a mouth on him for sure that needs to be checked at times.

Sitting on the couch waiting to hear from anyone at this moment, never being away from my children has my nerves freaking out.

Ready to get up and find my kids there's a soft knock on the door before the woman I know as Ella comes into the house with another very pretty woman behind her similar dark hair but definitely not related hers was much darker.

"Hello Remi-Rain how are you?" Ella says looking me in the eyes so gently.

"I am fine Ella thank you" I realize it sounded harsher than I intended. My social skills are rusty.

She walks over looping her arm with mine leading us back to the couch to sit. The other woman follows.

"Now let's get to know one another. It has been a trying few weeks and I believe we can help each other" Ella has a true mother's voice that calms me so easily.

Ember comes to life inside me, coming to the surface to greet our company. She wishes to speak.

"Let's begin" Ember speaks smoothly using my lips

Ella gave me a perfect full smile with joy.

I must start rebuilding instead of burning my bridges.

"Let's get some coffee. I have a story to tell" she says before leaving to the kitchen.

Epilogue

Silas POV

Exhaustion is starting to set into my bones. Aches and pains plague every inch as I make my way up to the medical room the pups are currently being examined in. This feeling of fatigue and pain is foreign to me.

With all of the renovations to the throne room as well as the small medical area within the pack house, it has been alot to get done on top of handling details on Zaden's transfer and making sure the feral she wolf and her family have everything they need.

"We are what she needs" Abraxis putting his opinion into my rampaging thoughts. "Maybe even a slap on that sweet ass"

The last comment made me smirk and grumble out a chuckle. The thought of my hands running all over her thick curves makes my pulse quicken, adjusting myself in my sweat pants to not be so obvious that my thoughts have been muddied with her images.

"We have not held a proper conversation with the female. Steps must be taken lightly, it is unclear what emotional damages she holds as well as if she is my true mate. The feeling comes and goes." At my words Abraxis is in agreement.

My dreams are filled with so many complicated scenes. One moment I am embracing this beautiful warrior woman in such an intimate embrace. Her hair in my hands and my lips assaulting her body, melts into a flicker of bloody, cries of torture that was flooded into my mind the day I ran after her.

Those must be her memories. I spoke to my parents and beta about the unwilling attack to my mind of all those gruesome pictures and films. We all agreed she somehow unwilling showed me her past in an attempt to stop me in my tracks. She was successful.

Reaching the medical area I can smell the male that she called Jake as well as the children. Taking a deep breath not knowing what to expect. I knock and enter the small room.

The first thing I see is almost comical if I was not so exhausted.

The male is crouching down talking to the small boy. His red hair slightly in his small furious face with balled up fists at his sides pointing at the large male in front of him.

"I want to go back to Mom right now! I'm sick of all these pokes from doctors and stupid questions bring us home!" The child demands with such power I felt it. This boy was a force indeed.

From the corner of the room a very small girl alot smaller than her brother, huffed her annoyance with no intentions of hiding her irritation. Sitting sideways in the recliner she yells across the room.

"Aleric! We can go when it's done! Jeez put some ice on that hot head! Goddess help us all!" Dramatically dropping her arms to hang off the black chair.

" Can I offer some assistance in making this faster?" My voice echoes in the space.

The male or Jake, stands up and walks over to me with his hand out and neck to the side to show respect. Firmly I grab his hand to shake and proceed to move to see the pups frozen in place. Abraxis immediately feels protective and wants to sooth the friction in the air.

"Alpha King Silas I am Beta Jacob Long of the Black Forrest Pack, I apologize for the time it has taken to conduct the exams. The pups have never been to a proper physical and are not familiar with normal pack life" Jake blurts out confident with a hint of caution.

The firey red head walks over and sticks his hands out. Confused at first I took both hands realizing the pup was trying to introduce himself and gave me both hands instead of one.

"Alpha King I am Aleric Rupert Astrid, son of my mom Remi, I am uncomfortable with all these ppl asking Soo many questions. Please let us go home" Alerics voice was strong and never stuttered.

I fought back a smile. He was confident and honestly so adorable. An odd sense of price spread through me. The Beta watching attentively.

"Hello Aleric, I apologize for how this has made you feel this way. This is something we have to do and sometimes we have to do things we are not happy with but must do. Now how about I ask you and your sister all the questions quickly and get this all over with?" I let some of my aura spread, not enough to scare just enough to show authority. The boy nodded and released my hands

The tiny girl has made her way over and followed her brothers actions, I take her teeny hands in my rough large ones. Her eyes so blue and large, filled with fear. She forces a smile.

"Hello Alpha my name is Nora Rain Astrid, I am 2 and my favorite color is Orange like fall leaves. I don't want to be a scardey pup." Nora's words coming out so sweetly.

" How about we get this over with so you can go back to your mom? I won't let anything happen you're safe Ms Nora" Waving in the doctor and giving the girl my hand back.

Mind linking my beta that I will be busy for a bit and to let the others know to push the evening meeting out a week or so. I think some time to process the information my mother is giving Remi and time for the pups to adjust from this necessary intrusive meeting.

Busy with my thoughts I almost missed the sound of Abraxis huff a sigh of contentment. Something about these small beings are relaxing my demonic beast. Melting my cold heart.